Who's in the Castle?

by Sue Graves

Illustrated by Gwyneth Williamson

FRANKLIN WATTS
LONDON•SYDNEY

First published in 2011 by
Franklin Watts
338 Euston Road
London
NW1 3BH

Franklin Watts Australia
Level 17/207 Kent Street
Sydney
NSW 2000

A CIP catalogue record for this book is available
from the British Library.

ISBN 978 1 4451 0280 1 (hbk)
ISBN 978 1 4451 0286 3 (pbk)

Series Editor: Jackie Hamley
Editor: Melanie Palmer
Series Advisor: Catherine Glavina
Series Designer: Peter Scoulding

Printed in China

Franklin Watts is a division of
Hachette Children's Books,
an Hachette UK company.
www.hachette.co.uk

CR-03/11

ABERDEEN
CITY LIBRARIES

Archie and Meg were going to a castle.

Archie was not happy.

"This castle is boring," he said.

"It's not boring at all!"
said Meg.

Then Archie saw
the wizard.

10

The wizard changed
Meg into a jester.

But no one
else noticed.

13

He changed her
into a monster.

But no one
else noticed.

He changed her into
a wobbly jelly.

But no one
else noticed.

It was time to go home.
But Meg was still a jelly.

"Help!" said Archie. "Please change Meg back now."

The wizard waved his wand. Then he was gone!

"You were right, Meg," said Archie. "The castle wasn't boring at all."

Puzzle Time!

Put these pictures in the right order and tell the story!

bored

happy

fed up

excited

Which words describe Meg
and which describe Archie
at the start of the story?

Turn over for answers!

Notes for adults

TADPOLES are structured to provide support for newly independent readers. The stories may also be used by adults for sharing with young children.

Starting to read alone can be daunting. **TADPOLES** help by providing visual support and repeating words and phrases. These books will both develop confidence and encourage reading and rereading for pleasure.

If you are reading this book with a child, here are a few suggestions:

1. Make reading fun! Choose a time to read when you and the child are relaxed and have time to share the story.
2. Talk about the story before you start reading. Look at the cover and the blurb. What might the story be about? Why might the child like it?
3. Encourage the child to retell the story, using the jumbled picture puzzle as a starting point. Extend vocabulary with the matching words to characters puzzle.
4. Give praise! Remember that small mistakes need not always be corrected.

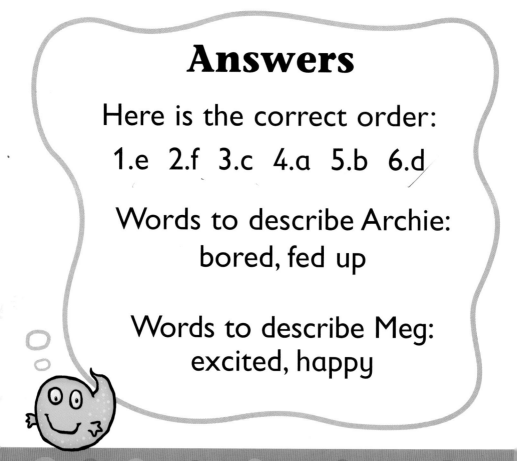

Answers

Here is the correct order:

1.e 2.f 3.c 4.a 5.b 6.d

Words to describe Archie:
bored, fed up

Words to describe Meg:
excited, happy